The Wit of
Tenali Rama

CONTENTS

Foreword

Tenali Ramakrishna, popularly known as Tenali Rama and the tales surrounding his wit and intelligence has become a household name for most kids today!

Born in a village in Andhra Pradesh, Tenali grew to up to become what he was popularly called–a 'vikata kavi' or a clown-jester-poet. Tenali Ramakrishna was more than just a minister in the court of Sri Krishna Deva Rayalu or Krishnadeva Raya, among other rulers in the Vijaya Nagar kingdom. He was a man with wit, originality and flexibility. He proved his wit by defeating the wits of eminent poets, learned men and the King himself. On such occasions, he would rely on his own resourcefulness.

Tenali Ramakrishna was one among the Astadiggajas or the eight poets who helped take Telegu literature and culture to a level less imagined with the introduction of the 'Prabandh' style of literature where poets used small stories from the Puranas to carve major kavyas. In fact, Krishnadeva Raya's (1509-1529) reign has been regarded as the Golden Era for history books where the eight authors together with Tenali Rama flourished with their poetic prowess to be known as the pillars of literary assembly.

As a child, Tenali Rama was lively and mischievous and could always look at the funny side of things. Recognising his natural skills of combining verse with humour, Tenali grew up to practice and compose poetry with diligence. His tales form an important part of Indian folklore and he is also a celebrated scholar of various languages like Telegu, Tamil, Kannada and Marathi.

Tenali's first taste of success!

The Royal Court of King Krishna Deva Raya of Vijaya Nagar, which was called the 'Bhuvana Vijayam', was extremely popular. Poets and scholars from all over the country wanted to have a place there. Tenali Rama, too, aspired to be a part of King Krishna Deva Raya's court. So, he approached the royal priest, Thathacharya and impressed him with his intellect and his skill at poetry.

On being promised to be introduced to the great king, Tenali waited anxiously for the day to come but it didn't.

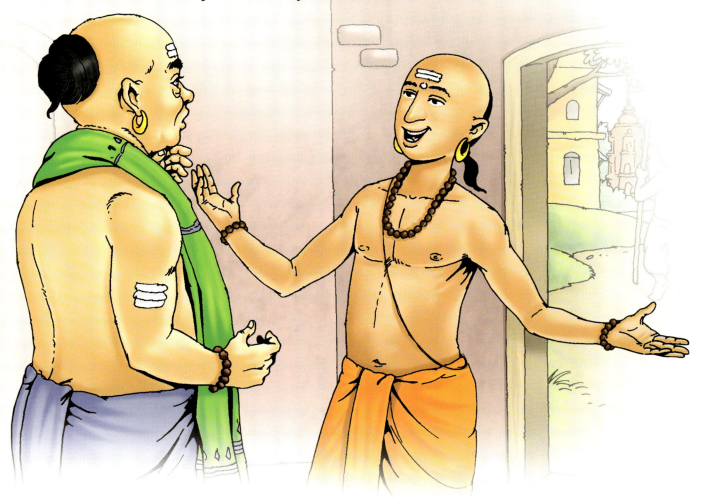

Upon hearing this, King Krishna Deva Raya was greatly impressed. Tenali was quick witted, humorous and confident, and seeing this, the King offered him a seat at the Royal court. This marked the beginning of his successful career as a minister, poet and court-jester at the Vijaya Nagar Kingdom, where he would later grow to become one of the King's most trusted advisors.

Tenali Outwits the Thieves

It was a dry summer for the people of the Vijaya Nagar kingdom that year. Not only that, the kingdom was also overrun with thieves.

One night, as Tenali Rama was glancing out of his window, he saw that his garden had become very dry – the land had become parched and his plants were dying in the scorching sun. Suddenly, his eyes caught two men hiding behind a tree.

At once, Tenali realised that they were thieves and that they were planning to rob him. "I will not let them escape this time," thought Tenali as he quickly thought of a plan to capture them.

Pretending as if he had not seen the thieves, Tenali stood by the window and said to his wife, as loudly as he could, "My dear, have you heard about the robberies that are taking place across the kingdom? We must be very careful. Let us put all our precious jewels inside a box and I shall throw it inside the well outside. The thieves will never be able to find it there."

He then turned to her and whispered, "There are thieves outside, let us catch them and teach them a lesson."

Tenali's wife understood and then hurriedly started to gather all their valuables and pretended to keep it all in a box. Tenali took the box, dashed out of the house and then threw the empty box delicately into the well, as if to protect the jewels from falling. After that, Tenali went back inside the house and shut the door.

Not long after Tenali and his wife had gone to sleep, the thieves were outside by the well, excited that Tenali had already shown them exactly where all his valuables were. They waited till everything was quiet and soon started drawing pails and pails of water out of the well. They drew... drew... drew and drew out water all night, while Tenali and his wife slept peacefully. This way, as the thieves were busy drawing out water, they were also watering his garden.

Next morning, Tenali Rama awoke to find the thieves still drawing water from the well. He saw that the garden was no longer dry and parched like before and that the water had flowed even to his flowerbeds. He was very happy to see this.

Laughing at the thieves and their foolishness, he yelled, "Do you really think that you can draw all the water out of that well? Or am I foolish enough to throw all my wealth into a well?"

Hearing this, the thieves realised that they had been tricked. Falling at Tenali's feet they begged for forgiveness.

Tenali forgave them and told them that he would not report them to the king only on one condition – that they promise never to steal again and that they would leave the Vijaya Nagar kingdom at once. The thieves, happy that their lives were spared, quickly agreed and ran away as soon as they could.

As for Tenali, he was happy to see his garden come back to life.

16

Babur Puts Tenali to Test

Tales of Tenali Rama's quick wit and intelligence had spread far and wide and King Krishna Deva Raya was very proud to see that the eight poets or Astadiggajas of his Royal Court were extremely popular throughout the country. King Babur, the ruler of Delhi, too had heard of the stories of the Astadiggajas especially the famous poet and court-jester of the Vijaya Nagar Kingdom.

Keen to test him, the great Mughal King invited Tenali to his kingdom. Upon receiving the invitation, King Krishna Deva Raya was pleased and sent him to visit the Sultan immediately. "But remember," said the King before Tenali set off for the Mughal Palace, "You must make the kingdom of Vijaya Nagar proud." Promising his King that he would not let him down, Tenali started out on his journey.

When Tenali Rama reached Delhi, he was greeted with honour and respect at the Delhi durbar. Yet, as he started narrating some stories, he noticed that there was not even a smile, let alone laughter, in the entire court. Tenali Rama was surprised to see this. All his attempts to make them laugh through various tactics and tricks failed.

This continued for fifteen days, and Tenali Rama was drained. He was puzzled as to why the King and his courtiers would not even chuckle at his stories. He then realised that the King must have ordered his courtiers not to laugh, for it was impossible for anyone to sit through any of his tales without laughing.

"Indeed," thought Tenali Rama,

"The King is trying to test me! I must try to figure out a way to catch his attention somehow."

On the sixteenth day, instead of going to the durbar, Tenali decided to follow the Sultan on his daily routine. He decided to do so under disguise so that the Sultan would not know that Tenali Rama was following him.

Tenali Rama noticed that the King went on a stroll along the banks of Yamuna River every morning and gifted gold coins to the poor. Suddenly a perfect plan to get the Sultan's attention once and for all, struck him. He rushed back home, excited about the plan that he would carry out the following day, and slept peacefully that night.

Early next morning, Tenali went to the same spot where he had seen the King the previous day. He went disguised as an old man holding a sapling in his hands. Seeing the King coming towards him, he sprung into action and started planting the sapling.

Seeing such an old man planting a tree, the Sultan asked him, "Old man, you won't live long enough to enjoy the fruits of this tree you are planting!"

Tenali replied, "Your Majesty, I have already enjoyed the fruits from the trees planted by my ancestors. This tree will bear fruits to be enjoyed by others in the future." Impressed with his reply, King Babur gave the old man a bag of gold coins.

20

"Your Majesty you are very kind. People get the fruits when the tree has grown but you have given me the fruit of my efforts even before I have planted the sapling." Thrilled with the old man's words, King Babur took out another bag of gold coins and gave it to him.

Not losing a minute, the old man said, "Oh, Your Majesty, this tree will bear fruits once every year but you have filled my arms with fruits of joy twice already."

Delighted with his wise words, the King gifted the old man with a third bag of gold coins.

21

At this point, the prime minister accompanying the King realized that the old man was very wise and advised the king to proceed further lest he emptied his coffers on this one man alone.

King Babur laughed and was about to walk away when the old man said, "Your Majesty, will you please give me a look?" On turning, the King and his prime minister found Tenali standing with the beard in his hands. Shocked but pleased at Tenali Rama's prank, King Babur honoured the wise minister with many rewards and gifts and sent him back with more for his King.

King Krishna Deva Raya was very happy that Tenali Rama not only proved his skills, but had also made his heart swell with pride.

The Royal Parrot

One bright sunny day, King Krishna Deva Raya went for a walk in his private garden with his favourite minister, Tenali Rama. The Royal gardens looked beautiful with the birds twittering on the fruit laden trees and the sweet fragrance of the flowers filled the air. The King couldn't stop admiring his surroundings as Tenali Rama looked on.

After a nice long walk, they headed back to the palace to see the King's most cherished friend, the Royal parrot. The parrot had its own room in the palace. Its cage was made of gold and was decorated with all kinds of precious stones. It had a diamond necklace around its neck and the floor of the cage was carpeted with a lush Kashmiri spread. A silver water bowl shimmered with the rays of sun and a golden bowl filled with berries and nuts was placed near the feet of the Royal parrot.

On reaching there, they were both shocked to see it screeching wildly. This worried the king terribly. It was swinging to and fro with its tiny feet carelessly perched on a golden swing laid inside the cage.

So, King Krishna Deva Raya took it out from its cage and allowed it to perch on his arm. Tenali Rama watched the King intently trying to soothe the bird. Seeing this, the king asked, "What are you thinking? Isn't my friend a real beauty?"

Tenali paused for a moment and then spoke, "I think that your friend might not be so happy here, my Lord."

"Not happy? But it has everything," said the king in fury. "What more could it need?"

25

As usual Tenali anwered humbly, "Forgive me, My Lord. But I think he needs freedom. We must not forget that the sky is his home." Annoyed at Tenali's comments, he shouted, "Never show me your face again Tenali," and he walked away.

Thereafter, the king couldn't be seen at court, for the Royal meals. Even the courtiers were frightened to go near him.

The next morning, King Krishna Deva Raya ordered the courtiers to serve him his meal. While he was eating, there was a knock at the door. The guard opened the door and was shocked to see a man with a earthen pot over his head. The pot had two holes from which a pair of eyes were peeping out. The king was startled and confused at the same time.

"Who are you stranger?" asked King Krishna Deva Raya. "It's me, Tenali Rama, My Lord," was the reply. Angry, the king shouted, "Tenali, how dare you disobey my orders! Didn't I tell you not to show me your face again?"

"Indeed you did My Lord. That is why I have this pot over my head to cover my face – so you would not see my face," answered the witty minister.

When the king heard this, he burst out laughing. Thrilled at his humour, the king ordered him to take the pot off his head and resume his seat at the court.

The king had a hearty meal, and he asked Tenali Rama to go for a walk with him to his private garden once again. Tenali accompanied him and was glad to see that the King had taken his advice.

"Forgive me, Tenali. You are right. The sky is his real home," said the king, setting the Royal Parrot free.

The List of Fools

King Krishna Deva Raya of Vijaya Nagar was very fond of horses. He was keen on owning some of the best steed in the country. One day, a horse trader visited his kingdom.

"Your majesty, I have the best Arabian steeds in the world. Would you like to see one?" asked the horse trader to the King.

The King looked over the trader's shoulder and saw a stallion. At one glance, King Krishna Deva Raya acknowledged the horse's beauty and immediately wanted it for himself. The horse trader asked, "Isn't he a beauty Your Majesty?"

"Yes indeed," said the King. "But I want more horses. When can you get them at the earliest?" asked the King excitedly.

"Well, it will take about two weeks to get them all for you, but you need to pay for them now," said the trader to the King. "Here you go, five thousand gold coins for the purchase of a whole lot," said the King.

Assuring the King of the delivery and thanking him, the trader set off with the horse leaving King Krishna Deva Raya excited and anxious for the following two weeks.

After two weeks had passed by, the king got extremely restless. The horse trader had not returned. One day, as he was walking in his garden wondering whether the horses would come or not, he noticed Tenali Rama sitting in the garden and scribbling something on a piece of paper.

Curious to know what he was writing, he asked Tenali, "What are you writing Tenali?" But Tenali gave no reply and continued to scribble.

King Krishna Deva Raya realised his mistake of trusting the horse trader. He also understood that his wise minister was trying to warn him of such dubious traders who would rob him. So he stopped worrying over the Arabian steeds and thanked Tenali for opening his eyes.

The Ambitious Barber

Every morning, the royal barber's task was to give King Krishna Deva Raya his daily shave. One morning, when the barber came to shave the King's beard, he found him asleep. Without waking the king up, the barber continued to do his job.

He did his job with such skill and accuracy that the King continued to sleep, undisturbed.

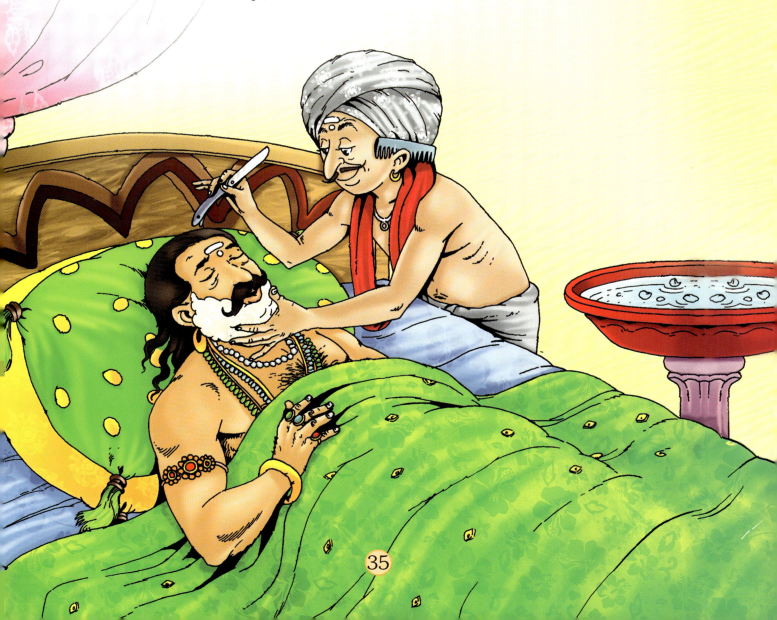

When the King awoke, he found that the barber had already shaved his beard. Amazed and impressed by the barber's ability with which he performed his duty, the King decided to reward him.

So, he asked the barber, "Ask for anything you want, young man and I promise that you shall have it!"

When the barber heard this, he was thrilled.

"Your Majesty, I have always wanted to serve you as Minister in the Royal Court. Would you allow me this position as a reward?" asked the barber.

"Indeed," replied the King, without really thinking of the consequences.

However, when the news of the barber reached the other ministers, they were not happy. They felt that an uneducated person was most likely to misuse his powers when promoted to such a high position.

So, they approached Tenali and narrated the entire story. Tenali too, concluded that the King had made a hasty decision and so, he decided that something must be done to make the King realise his mistake.

Back at the court, the King ordered the barber to step down from his position.

Filled with guilt because of his actions, the King said, "Ask for anything else, skilled one, but I cannot give you the position that you have asked for."

"Master you are kind and I don't need anything else," he replied and left for home.

King Krishna Deva Raya thanked Tenali Rama and honoured him with gifts, realising that nothing could match up to his intelligence and loyalty towards the kingdom of Vijaya Nagar.

Tenali Nabs the Diamond Thief

One morning, as King Krishna Deva Raya of Vijaya Nagar Kingdom was sitting with his courtiers and ministers at court, a servant came forth and begged to meet the King. The servant's name was Ramu and he had travelled far to meet the King.

"Your Majesty, I have come to seek justice," cried Ramu. The King asked Ramu to narrate his story.

"It was a hot day and…" started Ramu. "Cut it short!" yelled the King.

"I was accompanying my master to town one day. A sudden dust storm arose and we had to take shelter in an old temple," said the servant, as he was trying to hurriedly tell his tale.

"And then, all of a sudden, I saw a blue purse lying on the ground. So I picked it up and I opened it and I found sparkling diamonds!" continued the servant.

"What next?" asked a minister, who was enjoying the story.

"I showed them to my master and asked him if we should give it to the King, but he asked me to keep quiet about it."

"What did you do with the diamonds?" asked another minister.

"My master said that we should go back home and divide the diamonds among ourselves but he never gave me my share. So, I have come to you for justice."

43

The King, determined to get to the bottom of this immediately summoned Ramu's master to the court. The master came along with three witnesses. The master said, "Your Majesty I sent Ramu to deposit the diamonds at the state treasury and show me the receipt when he returned. But he came and complained to you. If he has not deposited the diamonds he should be punished."

At this point, the King did not know who to believe and so he called for the law minister and his wise court jester, Tenali Rama.

"We do not have proof against either of them," thought Tenali Rama. Then he took some time to think and said, "I have a plan but both of you will have to hide behind this curtain for a few minutes."

The King agreed and Tenali Rama started interrogating the three witnesses one by one.

He asked the first witness, "Did your master give Ramu the diamonds in front of you?" "Yes, Your Majesty," said the witness.

"Do you know the colour of the diamonds?" he asked the trembling witness.

"I just remember that the purse was blue, Your Majesty," said the witness.

Then, telling him to stand aside, Tenali moved on to his second witness.

"Did your master give Ramu the diamonds in front of you and can you tell me the colour of those diamonds?"

"Yes, Your Majesty. They were red," he replied looking at the first witness.

Finally, Tenali asked the third witness, "Did your master give Ramu the diamonds in front of you and if yes do you remember the colour of the diamonds?"

"They were white, Your Majesty," he replied glaring at the first two trembling witnesses.

Hearing this, the King pushed aside the curtain and realised who the culprit was. He screamed at the witnesses for conspiring against Ramu and helping his master. The four were then put behind bars and the servant, Ramu was set free.

And then he thanked Tenali, for they would have never nabbed the diamond thief if not for him.

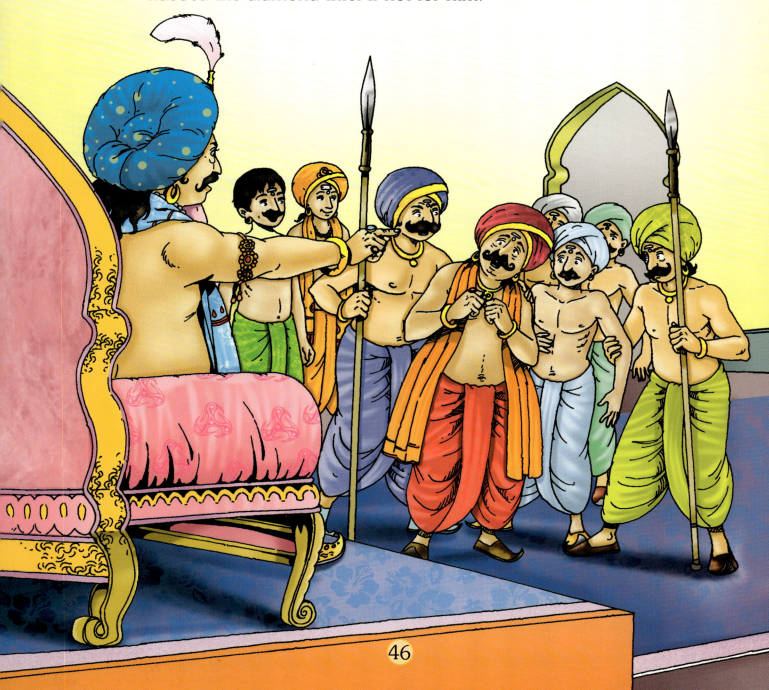

The Secret of the Invisible Fabric

One day, a beautiful woman entered the court of King Krishna Deva Raya and pleaded to meet with the King. "I can make divine fabric for the King," said the lady. She exhibited pleasing manners and behaviour and so, the courtiers granted her permission to meet with the King.

In the presence of the King, she stretched her hands as if to display a delicately woven fabric before his eyes and said, "Your Majesty, I have with me a divine group of individuals who can weave similar delicate and thin fabric. This fabric can only be seen with pure eyes."

The King was curious as to why this woman has come to him.

"What do you want from me?" asked the King.

"Your Majesty, such fabric has never been seen in the world. We have come here for your blessings, support and funds to carry out this task. This will be a fine discovery for the kingdom," she said.

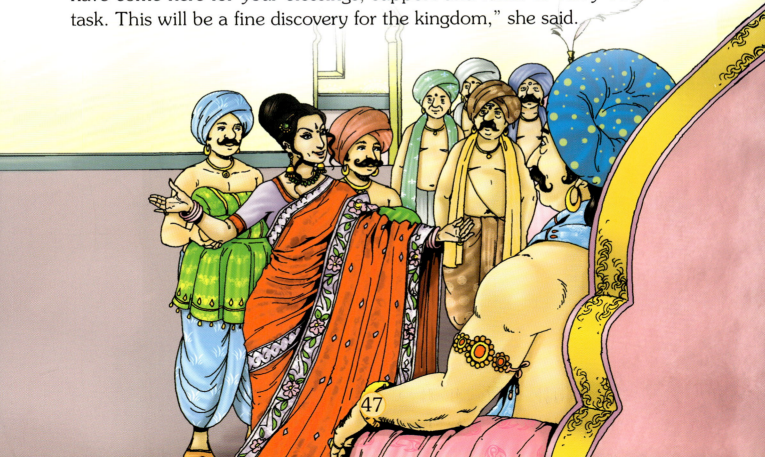

47

King Krishna Deva Raya believed the lady and was pleased with the idea. So he agreed to provide the funds to the beautiful lady and her divine weavers. He bade her to finish weaving the divine fabric in one year and the lady agreed.

A year passed by and there was no news from the lady and the weavers about the celestial fabric. So, the King sent some of his men to enquire about the weaving of the fabric. When the men reached there, they were shocked! They saw that the room of weavers had nothing – bare looms with no threads at all. However, everyone moved their hands frantically in a motion that looked like they were actually weaving.

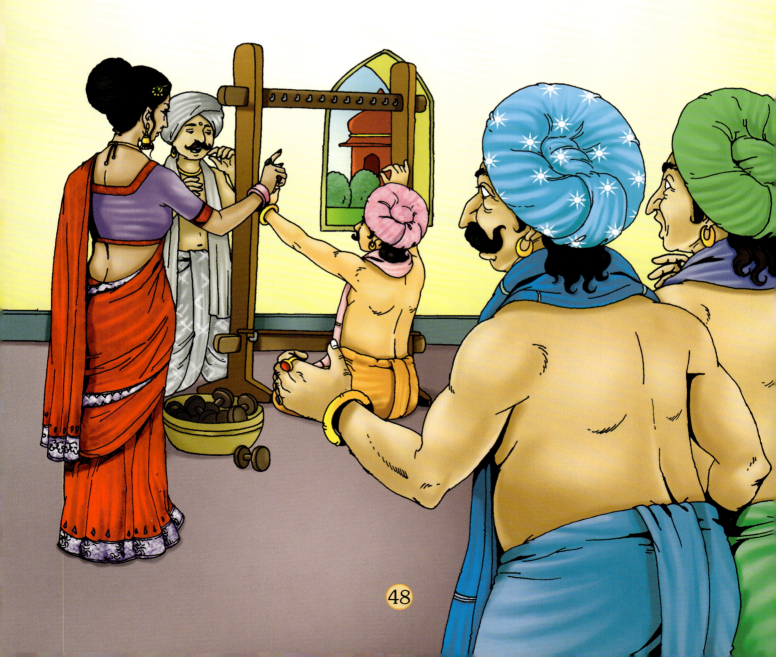

When the beautiful lady saw the courtiers, she walked up to them and said, "Gentlemen, is your king ready to see the celestial fabric?" Showing the exquisite fabric to the men, she said, "This fabric is only visible to those who are pure, I'm sure you can see it too?"

Nobody said a word because they couldn't see anything. Scared at being labelled sinners, they nodded their heads to say yes.

"The King must see your divine creation right away," said one rushing to tell the King.

49

When the lady reached the palace with her co-workers, the whole court was in silence, seeing that there was no cloth. Amidst the whispering ministers and courtiers, she explained,

"This celestial fabric is made of divine materials and is meant only for pure eyes! Do you see it?"

Afraid of being thought of as impure, everyone started praising her and screamed out aloud, "Yes!"

The King however, was confused. Turning towards his most faithful minister, he said in a whisper, "I'm afraid I cannot see the divine fabric, Tenali. Does that mean I am impure?"

"Surprisingly, I can't see it either Your Majesty. I think they are cheating us," replied Tenali.

Convinced that those people were cheats, Tenali comforted the King and told him that he would do something.

Tenali walked up to the beautiful lady and said, "If I may, lady?"

"Of course, young man," was the reply. "Are you confused at what you see or maybe don't see?" asked the woman, tauntingly.

"Not confused for a moment. In fact, I think this celestial fabric would look more beautiful if you wore it. Can you be kind enough to wear it for the King?" asked Tenali, confidently.

When she heard this, she understood that Tenali knew that she was trying to cheat the King and fool all the courtiers. She knew that there was no way that she could wear the cloth as there was no cloth! She knew that she now had to speak the truth. So, she fell on her knees and confessed her crime.

King Krishna Deva Raya banished the lady and her divine group from the Vijaya Nagar kingdom and rewarded Tenali for his intelligence in unfolding the secret of the invisible fabric.

52

A Handful Grain

Simhapuri was one of the major towns in the Vijaya Nagar kingdom. In this town, there lived a beautiful lady called Vidyullatha. This lady was famous for her beauty and skills which she possessed in dance, music, prose and poetry.

One fine morning, as people passed by Vidyullatha's house, they noticed a sign board that read, "One Thousand Gold Coins Will Be Gifted to Those Who Can Win with the Lady of the House in Wit, Poetry and Intellect." This sign board became a prestigious issue for most of the scholars and poets in town. Everyone wanted to confront Vidyullatha and win the one thousand gold coins.

Many people tried to meet the challenge but nobody could defeat the lady. This went on for days and days till people started losing hope of ever defeating her, till one day, Vidyullatha heard a firewood vendor selling firewood right outside her house.

"Firewood... strong firewood for sale," yelled the vendor, at the top of his voice. He stood outside her house and kept on shouting the same thing over and over again till Vidyullatha got annoyed by his yelling and went barging out of the house. She then yelled back at the firewood vendor, saying, "Stop it and tell me how much will a load of firewood cost?"

The vendor put down his load and said, "I will not sell this for money Madam. I will sell the entire load if you give me just a handful grain."

Irritated at the vendor, Vidyullatha said, "I heard you. Now just dump the load in the backyard and come here."

The firewood vendor stressed again, "Madam, please remember. I just want a handful grain. I will not bargain for anything else."

Fuming, the lady said, "You may be deaf but I am not. You fool, come here fast and take what you want."

Unloading the entire heap of firewood in the backyard, the vendor returned to her doorstep and said, "Madam, I don't want you to make a mistake. I just want a handful grain and nothing more or less. If you are not able to pay for it, you will have to give me one thousand gold coins and you will also have to tear out the hoarding outside your house."

"What nonsense?" said Vidyullatha in anger!

"It's not nonsense, Madam. You promised a price for the load of firewood and if you cannot keep your word, you will have to do as I say," the vendor replied.

Vidyullatha was irritated and so was the vendor. Both argued till huge crowds gathered and wondered why a rich and an intelligent lady like her was fighting with a poor vendor. Finally, the two decided to go to court.

When they came before the judge, Vidyullatha said, "My Lord, this man is crazy. I agreed to pay him a handful of grain for the entire load of firewood. But he insists that if I cannot give him what he wants, that is, a handful grain, then I should give him one thousand gold coins. I seek justice."

The vendor then spoke up. "My Lord, what she is saying is correct. I just wanted her to be clear," the vendor said humbly.

"It was a handful grain I wanted Your Majesty, which means just one grain in one hand which she misunderstood for a handful of grains. And now, she is refusing to give me the gold coins Your Majesty," said the vendor, now smiling.

Vidyullatha was outwitted by a vendor. Accepting defeat, she went back home giving the vendor one thousand gold coins. The hoarding was also removed and the entire town of Simhapuri rejoiced at Vidyullatha's defeat to a firewood vendor.

Nobody however, came to know that the firewood vendor was none other than Tenali Rama who had been sent by the King to end the contest started by Vidyullatha.

59

Tenali Salutes the Donkeys

In the Royal Court of King Krishna Deva Raya lived a pious man called Thathacharya. He was the royal teacher and family priest to the King. The royal teacher had a strange habit which was greatly disliked by most people, especially the Smarthas (Smartha is a sect of Brahmins who follow the Vedas).

When outside his home, he would always cover his head and face with his cloak so as to avoid seeing the Smartha in the town. The entire kingdom wondered why he hated the Smartha so much. This behaviour of his annoyed and irritated the learned Smarthas. The Smarthas, however, were scared to go and speak about this to the King as they thought he might get angry for complaining against the royal teacher. So, instead of going directly to the King, they approached his favourite minister, Tenali Rama.

Upon meeting Tenali, they explained the situation to the wise minister, hoping that he would find out a way to stop this foolishness.

"The royal teacher treats us with hatred," said one of the Smarthas.

"We are all here to discuss a problem with you concerning Thathacharya, the royal teacher. The royal teacher has been behaving very badly towards the Smarthas and has been humiliating us regularly. We dare not go to the king directly as he may get angry if we talk about Thathacharya," said Dhurjhati, a Smartha.

Tenali Rama too, had noticed the behaviour of Thathacharya and did not approve of it. He was happy that some people at last had spoken against him and his cruel behaviour.

Assuring them he said, "I'll do my best to solve this problem. I too feel that everyone should respect each other in this kingdom. I will speak to the King about it soon," said Tenali convincing the Smartha.

King Krishna Deva Raya had also heard of Thathacharya's behaviour towards the Smartha's and did not like it. He was worried that Thathacharya's behaviour could lead to a communal divide in his

kingdom. So, he called Tenali Rama to discuss the problem. "You have to think of a way to end this. I am very disappointed with Thathacharya. He is the royal teacher and he treats others with humiliation," said the King in a low voice.

"You should be very careful in solving this case Tenali. Thathacharya is learned and respected. No one should know that I have appointed you to teach him a lesson for looking down upon the Smarthas," ordered the King. "I won't fail you, Your Majesty," guaranteed Tenali as he walked away thinking of a way to end the problem.

Next morning, Tenali Rama got dressed and left for Thathacharya's house. As he was entering the gates, he saw the royal teacher stepping out of his door. Noticing Tenali, Thathacharya fumbled for his cloak to cover his face and head. "Hello Master, I'm your favourite disciple. Why are you covering your face?" Tenali said insistently.

"Since you are my favourite, I will tell you a secret," said Thathacharya whispering to Tenali Rama.

"Yes Master, what is it?" Tenali asked in curiosity.

"The Smarthas are sinners. It is said that if we look at them, we will become donkeys in our next life. That is why I cover my face and head when I see them. Don't tell this to anyone," commanded the royal teacher.

"Never," promised Tenali as he walked away.

Several days passed and Tenali Rama was anxiously waiting for the right moment to teach the royal teacher a lesson. Finally, the day arrived. King Krishna Deva Raya, Thathacharya and his eight competent ministers and other reputed scholars visited a garden on the outskirts of the city.

On the way back, a herd of donkeys blocked their way. Tenali Rama decided to take advantage of the situation and sprung into action. All of a sudden, he went closer to the donkeys and started bowing before the donkeys and paid homage to them. Falling to the ground, he started mumbling prayers and saluted the donkeys.

"Are you crazy? Why do you salute the donkeys?" asked the King.

"Forgive me Your Majesty, but I am only saluting Thathacharya's family," Tenali replied still stooping before the donkeys.

"This donkey is Thathacharya's brother-in-law; that one is his grandfather and the one with spots is his father. I feel blessed to see them altogether here," said Tenali pointing at each one of them.

"I don't understand. Are you fond of donkeys?" the King asked, teasing his favourite minister.

"No, Your Majesty. The royal teacher mentioned that looking at a Smartha would make him a donkey in his next birth. You can ask him, Your Majesty." Tenali replied in absolute admiration.

"Is that true Thathacharya?" the King asked the royal teacher, now understanding what his witty minister Tenali Rama was indicating. "Yes it is true," said Thathacharya bowing his head in shame.

"This kingdom is for everyone and not for you or me alone," said the King assertively to the royal teacher.

Thathacharya asked for forgiveness and never covered his face or head when he saw a Smartha again. The King rewarded Tenali Rama for tackling the problem with intelligence and humour.

Tenali and the Brinjals

King Krishna Deva Raya had a private garden that he was very proud of. He had a variety of vegetables grown there. This time, it was a rare variety of brinjals he had got planted. One day, he invited all his ministers and courtiers to taste the delicious brinjals plucked and cooked from his garden. Everyone found them to be the tastiest brinjals they had ever had.

When Tenali returned home, he couldn't stop talking about the delicious brinjals to his wife. He talked about the brinjals so much that even his wife wanted to taste them.

"I too want to taste the brinjals from the King's garden," his wife pleaded. "How can I get them for you?" asked Tenali. Tenali tried explaining that it would cost him his life to steal from the King's garden.

"I don't care," his wife insisted.

Tenali did not want to disappoint his wife. Knowing the consequences and the King's wrath, Tenali finally mustered up the courage to steal one brinjal from the King's garden. He climbed over the walls and managed to pluck one for his wife

that night. She cooked a delicious meal and slept happily. Tenali on the other hand, sat up worrying all night. Tenali Rama's wife enjoyed the brinjals so much that the next day she insisted that he get two more brinjals so that she could prepare enough to feed their son. "Please get two brinjals. This is the last time I shall ask you this," she begged her husband.

"All right, but this is the last time I am going to steal for you," said Tenali angrily.

So Tenali Rama again went to the King's private garden. He climbed over the walls that night again and plucked two brinjals this time. Tenali knew that the King would find out

about the missing brinjals, and so, quickly thought of a plan to prevent him from finding out that it was Tenali. As his wife prepared the brinjals, Tenali ran up to the terrace and threw a bucket of water on his son who was asleep.

Carrying him inside he said, "Let us rush in my son, it is raining here." When dinner was ready, he fed his son and put him to sleep reminding him that if he had not got him inside the house in time, he would have fallen ill because of the rain.

Next morning, the King was taking a walk in his private garden. Here, he was informed by the royal gardener, who kept count of the number of brinjals that were growing in the garden that three brinjals were missing.

The King was furious and ordered his courtiers to find the thief. Soon, news spread about the missing brinjals as the King declared a prize on the thief's head.

The chief minister was suspicious only of Tenali Rama, for there was none as daring as he was in that kingdom and only someone bold could carry out the dangerous feat of stealing from the King's garden. He said to the King, "Your Majesty, I cannot think of anyone else but Tenali Rama, who would steal from your private garden."

King Krishna Deva Raya couldn't believe the chief minister at first but he grew suspicious because the thief could not be caught. The King said to the chief minister, "Tenali Rama is very clever. Let us call his son. We can find out the truth from the boy as Tenali would not teach his son to lie." When the child reached the court, the King asked the little boy, "What did you have for dinner my son?"

"My mother prepared delicious brinjals," replied the kid.

Tenali Rama was summoned to court and the chief minister accused him of stealing the brinjals. "You have disappointed me. You could have asked me for some instead of stealing them" said the King, angry and heartbroken.

"It is not true, Your Majesty," replied Tenali. "My son slept early last night and was having bad dreams the whole night because he has been talking rubbish since morning. He insists it rained last night," replied Tenali almost breaking into tears.

The King turned towards the child and asked, "How was the weather last night dear son?"

"It rained heavily and I got wet because I was sleeping on the roof," replied Tenali's son innocently.

The chief minister and the King apologised to Tenali for having accused him of stealing the brinjals, while Tenali returned home with his son swearing never to steal again.

The Most Difficult Job

King Krishna Deva Raya was very happy with the way he ruled his kingdom. One day, he said to his courtiers, "You are all wise and learned men seated here. Perhaps one of you can tell me, which is the most difficult job in this world?"

All of them had ready answers. "Your Majesty, ruling a kingdom is the most difficult task in this world," agreed everyone. They were scared to say anything else otherwise, it could make the King angry.

The King was pleased that his courtiers thought so highly of him. But his happiness was short-lived when he noticed Tenali Rama smiling to himself as if he found the anwer to be funny.

"Why are you smiling Tenali? Do you not agree with the rest of the courtiers that my job is the most difficult in the world?"

Rising hurriedly from his seat, Tenali said, "Indeed, you are right, Your Majesty. Although I do agree that it is difficult to rule a country but, I do not think that it is the most difficult job in the world. I think to be a mother and to keep a child happy is the most difficult job in this world."

Offended, the King said, "Prove what you have said, learned one."

So, the wise minister asked for a mother and child to appear in court. Stroking the child's head, Tenali Rama said, "Son ask the King for whatever you wish to have right now and he will get it for you."

"I want an elephant," said the boy innocently.

The King ordered that an elephant be given to the child.

The child at once commanded, "Put it in my basket because I want to show it to my friends." But that, of course, was impossible and so, the child started crying.

Everyone tried to console him and so did the King but nothing that anyone said would make him change his mind. Tenali too, tried to console him, but the child continued to cry. His mother too was scared and embarrassed. She looked at her son with glaring eyes but Tenali said, "Lady, can you fulfil your son's wish without shouting at him?"

The mother bent down to her son and said, comfortingly, "Son, here take this little toy elephant. The big one won't fit into your basket. How will you take it home?"

The little boy's tearful eyes gleamed as he looked at his mother happily. He stopped crying and started playing with the toy elephant.

81

Tenali ordered the mahout to take the elephant away. Before Tenali Rama could explain, the King said, wiping the sweat from his brow, "Certainly a mother's job is the most difficult job in the world."

Tenali Rama received many gifts from the King who commanded everyone to share their views just like Tenali Rama did.

Tenali and his Cat

Once upon a time, Vijaya Nagar kingdom was under the menace of rats. There were rats everywhere – closets, kitchen, bedrooms. They nibbled on everything possible; they ate books, wood, paper, food and clothes. King Krishna Deva Raya himself was fed up with the tiny creatures. Tired of seeing rats everywhere, even on his food, the King decided that strong measures need to be taken to get rid of the menace. So, the King ordered every household to raise cats – strong and healthy cats!

So each household started getting cats. The more the cats, the lesser the rats were in the Kingdom. The King was very proud that he had solved the rat problem. But, after a couple of days, people started complaining that their cats were consuming a lot of milk. So, the King gifted every house with cows so that there would be enough milk for the cats. However, Tenali Rama, the wisest of all the ministers in King Krishna Deva Raya's court thought it was a sheer squander to waste all the milk on a cat, though he too raised one out of respect for the King.

Every morning, Tenali would pour the boiled milk into a pan for his cat. One day, as he was pouring out milk for his cat into a pan, his cat rushed to take a sip but burnt its tongue and fled.

From then onwards, Tenali Rama noticed something strange – his cat would dash out of the door every time it was served milk. Eventually, the wise Tenali thought, rather than waste the milk, it was better to drink it himself. Days passed by and his cat grew lean and weak.

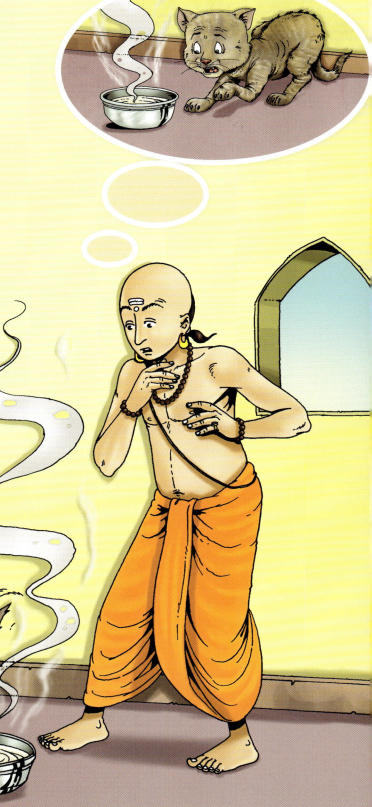

One day, the King ordered everyone to bring their cats to court. "I want to see if the cats are being fed well," commanded the King. He wanted to reward the master of the healthiest cat and punish those who didn't feed their cats well. When everyone assembled, he was shocked as well as disappointed to notice that it was Tenali Rama's cat which was the weakest and skinniest of all.

"Are you not feeding your cat well Tenali?" asked the King.

"Your Majesty, it seems like this cat does not like milk very much."

The King could not believe Tenali as it was impossible that a cat could run away from milk.

"Your Majesty!" said Tenali, "If you want you can offer milk to the cat and see for yourself." So, a bowl of milk was brought and, to the King's surprise, the cat fled away as soon as it caught sight of the milk.

"What did you do Tenali? Surely you must have done something that has made the poor cat dislike milk!" shouted the King.

"Your Highness, the first time I gave it milk, the milk was hot and it did not strike my mind that it would burn the cat's tongue. Indeed it did. Since it stopped having milk, it has turned out to be very good at catching rats!" exclaimed Tenali. "Let's not forget that that was the main purpose of raising the cats, in the first place,"
said the wise Tenali.

Finally, the King understood Tenali's point and let him go, without his scurrying cat.

The Key to Heaven

One day, as Tenali Rama was on his way, to King Krishna Deva Raya's court, he noticed there were a lot of people rushing somewhere. He stood there for sometime and wondered where those people were scurrying to and all of a sudden, overheard people talking on the streets, "This Sadhu can perform miracles. He sits at the temple and fulfils everyone's wish," said one man to another.

Tenali Rama grew curious about the new miracle man. He wanted to check for himself. So, he forgot all about going to the court and rushed towards the temple to see for himself what the sadhu was all about.

On reaching, he found huge crowds outside the temple. People came with gifts and offerings for the Sadhu.

"I hear he has the key to heaven," said an eager devotee to Tenali Rama.

"Really?" asked Tenali playing along.

"Let us see," he said with a frown.

The temple was crowded with people from all corners of the Kingdom singing hymns. Everyone pushed to get closer to the Sadhu, Tenali Rama, too, was among them.

The miracle session began and the Sadhu started chanting the 'shlokas'. Tenali was curious about this Sadhu so he was standing close to him and paying extra attention to what the Sadhu was saying and doing.

After a few minutes of chanting, Tenali noticed that the Sadhu kept repeating the same lines over and over again while the entire crowd followed in worship. He realised that he was a fraud and was fooling everyone.

Seeing this, Tenali decided to expose the fraud to the public. In order to do so, he needed to act fast. Grabbing a strand of hair from the Sadhu's beard, Tenali announced, "I have found my key to heaven! It lies in this strand of hair from the Sadhu's beard."

Before the Sadhu could react, the gathered crowd pounced on his beard to seek their key to heaven. Tenali Rama stood laughing, while the Sadhu ran to save his beard and his life.

The King heard of this incident and rewarded his minister for protecting the innocent people of his kingdom from the fake Sadhu.

Main Characters of Tenali Rama

King Babur

Thathacharya

Thimmanna

Beautiful Lady